NON SEQUITOR

NON SEQUITOR

By: Ella Kuzmenko

authorHOUSE®

AuthorHouse™
1663 Liberty Drive
Bloomington, IN 47403
www.authorhouse.com
Phone: 1-800-839-8640

Published by AuthorHouse   10/24/2012

ISBN: 978-1-4772-7437-8 (sc)
ISBN: 978-1-4772-7438-5 (e)

Library of Congress Control Number: 2012917928

First and foremost I thank God for all of my achievements in life—sometimes he uses a flashlight, sometimes a small match or even high beams but he always manages to shine a light toward the end of the tunnel no matter how rough the path ahead of me seems to get. I also thank my parents for constantly providing a roof over my head, three hot meals a day, three lovely siblings whom I love very much, and one of the most entertaining and enriching environments for learning and growing as a person.

And yet there is someone whom we seem to forget about a lot and always forget to thank for our accomplishments- the teacher. It still fazes me that the country built on innovation and creative thinking still maintains an average teachers' salary that is well below what it should be considering the implications educators have on the children of today who become the inventors of tomorrow. It was my teachers who doubled as safety guards during recess, parents in the afternoon and mentors throughout life that created an environment where my thoughts were fostered and imagination ran wild. Each and every one of you are who made me who I am today and I am forever in debt to you for the knowledge, wisdom and kindness you taught me. Thank you to every educator I have ever had. Thank you Mrs. Wilson, Mrs. Shoemaker, Mr. Cole, Mrs. Moses, Mrs. Anderson, Mrs. Young, Mr. Mann, Mr. Waters, Mrs. Lawrence, Mrs. Chapp, Mrs. Brownfield,

Mrs. Moon, Mrs. Anderson, Mrs. Thomason, Mr. Mueller, Mrs. Palumbo, Mrs. Riley, Mrs. Watt, Mrs. Alvarez, Mrs. Rayburn, Mr. Westerside, Mrs. Ito, Mrs. Black, Mr. Sampson, Mrs. Boyd, Ms. Pilochowski, Mrs. Hancok, Mrs. Palmer, Mrs. Peterson, Mrs. Curtis, Mr. Leffler, Madame Linder, Mrs. George, Mrs. Lynch, Mr. Hallock, Mr. Rao, Madame Linder, Mr. Duncan, Mr. Gingrich, Madame Linder, Mr. Ellsworth, Mrs. Grueber, Mr. Burress, Mr. Kincaid, Mr. Grimes, Mr. Rahr, Mr. Wood, Mr. Bright, Mrs. Krause, Mrs. Piper, Mrs. Misoda, Ms. Flikemma, Madame Le Guennec, Mr. Kendrick, Mrs. Dunda, Mrs. Ogimachi, Mrs. Klein, Greg Peszek, Jeffery Richards and Hemanth Srinivas.

And I apoligize for sleeping, talking, constantly disrupting, not participating, and chewing gum in your classes.

You cannot fix that which isn't broken

CAUTION

Meet Beatrice. In order to escape from the tormenting memories of her past Beatrice creates characters out of ink on the crisp white pages in front of her. When pen hits paper however she often wanders so far into her fictional universe that she is completely submerged by her creations. Join Beatrice on a journey with all the misfits she calls the characters of her life.

WHEN?

Most humans are too caught up in finding the deeper significance in the most insignificant of details so much that out of spite there shall be no label of time or place. This story could take place in the past, it could take place in the future—it could even be taking place in the present.

B

B is for beginnings.

BEGINNING

The truth is that in every story there is no beginning nor is there an end. Every story is just that; a story—a collection of moments made up of certain characters and events most likely for some higher purpose-. This is a story neither about love nor strife. It is neither of war nor peace. It mirrors exactly what it is attempts to depict; a series of very broken moments about a series of very broken characters.

H

H is for home. But H is also for Hell. And who knew sometimes they could be one in the same.

HOME

The past

There was little room in the pint sized space we called our kitchen but it was proportionally tucked away in the little birdhouse we called our house. Although the enclosing was petite Mother wouldn't have it any other way then to keep it impeccably tidy every second of my existence. Fresh lilacs were placed and replaced in a crystal vase every morning and a hospital white sheet covered the oval dining table for three. The third bear was never consistent with his dinner visits but nonetheless mother always set a place for him; in hopes things would change.

After we had said our prayer acknowledging our thanks to the Lord we sat down to sip our soup and watch the candle burn out slowly.

Just then interrupting our perfect silence we heard a gruff voice muffled by the door exclaim "why don't you just go to hell?!" A fumbling of the lock and twisting of the doorknob was followed by a final swinging open of the door. The gruff drunkard staggered in, cigarette in the corner of his mouth. He walked in a sort of zigzag pattern to his chair and took a seat without so much as a greeting or even a simple word of acknowledgment. He took the ladle and began to pour himself a steaming bowl of soup but Mother slapped his wrist and looked him straight in the eye.

"So what you think you can just leave us for four goddamn months to whore around with your filthy upstate sluts and come back and all is forgiven?" Ma growled at him her thick accent seeping through. My mouth gaped as I had never heard her talk with such vulgar language. If we went to a Country Club like those I hear about from the wealthy folks at school then the other mamas would outright say "that is no way for a young lady to be talking in this day and age!"

"Who the hell do you think you're talking to?" Jonathan says standing up to tower over mama.

"Well I know for sure I'm not talking to the man I married seven years ago! The one who *didn't* abandon his family! Then one who *used* to be welcome here!"

Jonathan responded in a softer voice, "If I'm not welcome here why's there three places set at the table, huh?" as he motioned towards his place setting.

Mama looked away quietly-she would never admit that since the perfect morning he walked out of that door every meal has been set with an extra place set for him. I guess Ma never truly expected him to come back because in her head she imagined that if he did; everything would suddenly be different.

"What the hell you lookin at kid?" He snapped in my direction. I hated that. Whenever he's drunk he acts like a goddamn maniac, a loony bird, a psycho. The worst part was that he always asked for my-

"Show me your grades kid." He shouts interrupting my thoughts. Bastard, I think. I feel so guilty for saying it I get my composition book in two times the normal speed and wait patiently for the storm to hit. It's been so long since the brutal monster had been back that I had almost forgotten this sick routine.

"Straight Ds?!" He hollers. But instead of taking a drunken swing at me, he places a greasy gruff hand on my head and suddenly I'm in the air hanging by the sole hairs on my head. I felt like the freshly chopped carrots Mama had chopped up earlier for our soup; being thrown into a boiling pot of water; crying out in terror. Wincing at the pain I feel a million sharp knives puncturing my already opened wounds. A second before darkness took me over I locked eyes with my father; a pair of lifeless pale blue eyes that looked so . . . surprisingly lost stared gravely back at me. The poor drunkard had no consciousness of what he was doing and I knew tomorrow he wouldn't recollect a single event from today; denying everything. And as I hung there in mid air for the slightest second I didn't feel sorry for myself; but for him. And then everything went pitch black.

HELL

Present

Isolated and secluded from the light of society. Packed away into a box without the chance to protest back he sits alone in a caged cell gasping for air. He's placed inside a square cubicle with only the darkness of the creeping nighttime and the faint light hovering overhead as his friend. The glow from the suspended lone light bulb is slowly flickering out as the shadows dance around him on the gray stone wall. He desperately clings onto the bars of the window, eyes wandering for a brighter answer but the darkness has already set in; painting a drape of night sky coated with brilliant twinkling stars and an unusually ostentatious moon. Plummeting back down to the cold hard floor of the prison cell a million thoughts race through the mind—questions arise of thoughts unspoken and memories unbroken. Confusion sets in as he braces himself for the hard blows he knows are up ahead. And as he lies alone and puzzled by the world it gives dawn enough time to slink up on him and send its gleaming rays upon his face early the next morning.

Heavy steps near closer and closer as every inmate rushes to the bars of their cubicle in hopes of the message being for them. Not wanting to move, so comfortable basking in the sun he lays there contently. But his sleep is cut short for the warden raps his knuckles on the steel gate once as a warning and proceeds to throwing open the door and pulling him outside for a visit. They shuffle away together through the dark halls that are adorned with snowy white cobwebs and forgotten paraphernalia. Finally the guard steers the old man into the bright flooding lights of the visiting room. There are a few hushed conversations taking place, the tones of the inmates drained and monotone. He sits himself down and a small girl sporting pig tails and a pastel yellow dress on the other side of the glass sprints over to him. She was named Eva-after her mother and she sits across from the old man in a navy blue folding chair, the grin erased from her face in a second as she overlooks her grandfathers' eyes. The crease in his forehead substantially deepening from each visit, as were the crinkles around his worn out eyes and frown lines on his face. His posture sagging a fraction more each time as he heaved his elbows onto the counter and pulled his face up enough to peek over at his granddaughter. Not wanting to look too long for fearing the memory would fade, yet not wanting to glance away too quickly for fearing it might be his last glimpse. The liquid began forming in his eyes, the quiver of his lip unstoppable in his mind as he reaches out his palm and gently places it on to the glass. His granddaughter, sitting just a foot away yet in reality is millions of miles away-not knowing this perfect stranger, and worse, not wanting to know him,—she pulls her palm forward too. They sit like that for a second, as he sheds his silent tears. Then after what feels like seconds a firm grip on his shoulder and a gruff voice murmurs "your times up son", and he knows he must go. He watches with sad eyes as the girl bounces off the chair and runs away into the hidden sanctuary of her mother's skirt. And as they turn to

HUMANITY

"Now Eva what did you write about today?" Mrs. Ryans, Evas shrink, asked as she looked at her intently studying every move Eva made.

Eva handed over a crumpled up piece of paper with a false sense of security.

"It's titled Humanity" she mumbled through her clenched teeth, never understanding the point of these weekly visits.

"Humanity" whispered Mrs. Ryans and her voice trailed off as she immersed herself in Evas poetry.

We all desire different ends

Never stopping to make amends

Following peculiar trends

Not seeing where our road bends

We all have our own private views

As we quietly sit in our church pews

Making silent oaths to never lose

And to never have to choose

And when we hear of the darkening news

Behind closed doors in agony we sip our booze

In terror we sit and muse

Pondering the aberration we wallow in our blues

Yearning to reject the deceivable abuse

We manufacture our plausible excuse

We omit and revolt in order to refuse

In the ends we just disorient and confuse

We all strive for different ends

But as the sun sets and the curtain slowly descends

We can attempt to fuse and somehow become friends

"I'll just add this to the uh collection. You may go now." Mrs. Ryans excused Eva and sat back in her chair attempting to grasp the reality in front of her.

L

L is for loopholes. L is also for Life because sometimes the very reason one is alive or stays alive-is because of a mere loophole.

LOOPHOLES

Past

"Children settle down!" crowed Mrs. Wilson at the rowdy students as they began returning back to their seats.

"For today's lesson we are going to learn all about" her voice droned on and on and as I attempted to not fall asleep on my perched up elbow. As soon as I felt myself salivating on my arm my eyes fluttered awake to Mrs. Wilson right in front of my face.

"Perhaps this year you could actually graduate this grade Eva" she snapped as she slammed a composition book on my desk.

Inhaling I opened it up and read the stupid prompt; "write about theatre and its significance." Luckily I was a bit cleverer than the other snot nosed kids in my class and I liked to think that it wasn't completely due to the fact that this was my second time in this grade.

I dipped my pen in ink and began my composition for the day.

"Theater", I wrote in big letters at the top of the page.

Theatre is not just for actors. Theatre is not just for the brilliant and the talented; theatre is what every human is enrolled in from the day they take their first breath. Life is a stage on which we are all acting every second, every minute and every day of our lives. We each have a role to play and just as our theatre teacher says "there are no small parts only small actors" because in truth every part is the same as any other, it is just a different mold of that part. And yet this theatre production is completely impromptu for our parts are not scripted and our acting is far from flawless, so far from perfection. Everything is extemporaneous; every action, every word, every laugh, every fight, every tear is completely unrehearsed. That is why humans are not perfect; because we don't have the chance for a practice run-we just go from the top and cross our fingers that everything will be okay.

"Oh stop trying to justify your imperfection" a voice booms behind me and I see Mrs. Wilsons hands tower over my page as she rips out my entry and crumbles it up into a ball.

Slapping my wrists with her ruler she yells, "pay attention to the *prompt* you can be original once you actually pass this class!"

As a few snickers are released from my dreadful classmates and I mumble an inaudible, "maybe I don't want to conform". And I dunk my pen into my inkwell and begin another entry; this time of satisfactory condition to the boss.

LIFE

Past

I inhale a deep breath.

"It's such as dark subject. A mothers worst nightmare, a sisters furthest thought, a brothers last curse, a fathers last cry. It's the one thing they don't teach you in Sunday school, let alone during your summer course of driving school. It was hardly the windows rolled down-hands in the air—music blasting out your eardrums—in the convertible scenario. It was a muggy morning with the clouds hung low over the evergreens and drops of liquid picking up speed to a heavy drizzle. A soft lullaby was whispering through the speakers and a murmuring motor soon put passenger number five straight to sleep. The wind slowed and music stopped and it was just us, driving into our destiny; the '73 pickups headlights our only light aside from the beautiful stars dancing in the night against the canvas of darkening sky. The road unravels from beneath us as we fly past the cabins with smoke huffing out their chimneys and forests of evergreen trees watching us from above. Life's crisp pixel perfect photographs faded into the ancient blurred images of tomorrow as we rushed past on the perfectly smooth highway of deaths touch. Rushing so fast, not breathing, and not stopping. And as every ride, there comes a time for it to stop. And the passengers must descend. We were almost comfortable, almost soothed, and almost content with the darkness enclosing upon us when the lights flooded our vision. We held onto that curtain of darkness so reliantly; the curtain that hid the moon and veiled the stars and let us feel content in our loneliness was our only barricade to reality. But the brightness of the deep golden glow was deathly unbearable to our bare eyes that had been so accustomed to the darkness around us. Once the rays shined upon us our eyes became blinded by the intensity of the brilliance of the shining light and we lost our sight; we lost our direction. His hands trembled as he blindly attempted to find the placement of his steering wheel that would drive him into his perfectly designed artificial future. Not able to reconnect with the reins that controlled his outcome he frantically cried out with a silent voice and shed his silent tears. Unable to retake control he waited in misery as the seconds dragged out into what felt like hours and he slowly felt the impact of the crash. He felt the slow drawn out collision of one vehicle hurling itself towards another; exerting an impossible amount of angry force. He could taste the vacant-ness in his mouth as the blood seeped from his perishable breath and stained his clothes; tarnishing his innocence. The collision dented the side of his steel vehicle of transportation and pinned his breath beneath its stone cold grasp and with that it tainted his existence on this earth; slowly and anguishingly robbing his life."

I exhaled. Looking up from beneath the lights hovering over me I catch almost every single one of my classmates paralyzed in fear.

"But he's still alive right?" asks a shaky voice in the back of the room.

"No, but that's not the point," I respond slowly.

"What was his name?" a quiet voice murmured.

"Did you know him?" another voice hollered.

"Why did you kill him?!" little Alex shrieked in the back of the room throwing his glue stick to the front of the room in hopes of hitting me.

As I duck from the throw I chuckle and respond coolly, "its fiction. It's imaginary. He's dead. But he never existed. The only life he had had been in a vacuum."

As little Alex began sobbing Mrs. Wilson looked at me angrily and grabbed me by the arm.

"Okay! Okay settle down pupils! Don't worry he survived! He's alive! Eva is going to go read her story to the principal now!" she attempted to calm the class down as she threw me out of her classroom.

Before I turned to walk to the office however she growls at me through clenched teeth, "keep your sick stories to yourself most of these children haven't even lost a goldfish let alone are capable of grasping the loss of a human being."

"Maybe it's time for the bubble to pop." I stormed off slamming the door with a hard thud on my way out.

K

K is for key. K is also knowing which key fits to which lock.

KNOWING

I never knew if I should envy or pity those kids. Those kids that heard the word and in their minds immediately envisioned a photo book of warm and vivid memories. Those kids that knew exactly what the word felt like, what it smelled like, and even what it tasted like. The kids that were always sheltered from the tragedy of reality because they always had the same familiar haven to hide in whenever the fierce wind blew a little harder or the storm outside didn't settle down in time. I knew that it would be the same kids that drew their invisible lines at the edge of town that would one day fall back into their perfect circle of cohesion so that the closest you could get would be as an outsider; constantly looking in.

Looking back now I think I always knew it, even if it was in the back of my mind, even if I didn't want to acknowledge it I always knew I was a nomad. There was never a night that I drifted off into sleep without a roof over my head, and yet there was never a day in my life that I understood the concept of home. I could write about it, I could even sing about it or pretend I understood it but the four letter word alluded me far worse than anything else I would ever come in contact with.

KEYS

"Did you have a nice visit at the museum?" Mrs. Ryans asked.

Eva stared at her in horror. "NICE?!" She hollered.

"Yes Judy, re-witnessing tragedy was very *very* nice!" She yelled sarcastically as she ripped out a piece of lined paper out of a tattered notebook and threw it at Mrs. Ryans who was still taken aback by the fact that Eva had used her first name-an unusual occurrence for her most calm and collected patient.

As Eva stormed out of her office Mrs. Ryans bent down and unraveled the paper. "Keys," the title read.

Keys

Tools that unlocked doors
Doors to cars that would drive them along highways
Driving them to work
Driving them home
Keys to doors of homes
Brightly lit homes waiting patiently for their
owners to return
Keys to doors of shops
Bread shops
Barber shops
Tobacco shops

Shops that fed
And shops that clothed one another
Their keys were confiscated
Thrown into a pile
Keys to locks
Locks that would rust up and never be opened again
Keys to nothingness
But within the camps
They found a different type of key
The key to survival
The key to hang on
The key to fight for their lives
And never give up
The keys of their lives.

Mrs. Ryans swallowed hard and dropped the piece of paper into her bin labeled "Patient: Beatrice".

M

M is normally for mother. But this story is far from normal.

gold. Her cheeks are freshly powdered with a slight hint of rosy pink on the cheekbones and a darker grey on her eyelids. She was even wearing a dab of jungle red on her fully plumped lips. She is slowly dissecting through the apples looking for just the perfect ones and as she is doing so her blouses top button undoes and I catch a glimpse of her lacy black and dark red bra that is attempting to support all of her cleavage which spills out more each time she leans over. I am gaping at the sight of her digging deeper in her apple hunt, and I am not the only one staring. The hot sun that is making the air so thick and humid got about five degrees hotter with the spectacle Madeline was making. A group of sixteen year old boys gathered around the coca cola coolers to get a better view. Madeline's tightly wrapped blouse was tucked into an even tighter pencil skirt that lay four inches about her knees. Her nylons were running all the way down into her monstrous six inch devilishly red heels. As she was bending over scouting for apples the whole world was silently agreeing there was no way she would eat them or anything else for that matter what with her petite figure and all. Madeline of course had to lean in just a bit further making her skirt rise even higher. The boys were hooting now and whistling. If Madeline hears or notices them she doesn't say so. She simply tosses a few more Granny Smiths into her forest green rucksack and stands smiling at me showing off her shiny white teeth. The way her curls ensconce her neck and flow down her front ending perfectly right above her breasts makes her seem like somewhat of an angel. So perfectly created, yet so deviously rotten on the inside; but no one would suspect a thing.

"How's Johnny?" She asks warmly, clutching an apple with both hands. I shrug, uncomfortable in my heavy Sunday dress under the blazing scorching sun.

"Eva!" Mother calls close by and I turn to see her rushing towards me. Madeline quickly turns and walks away her heels purposely shaking every part of her that she knows men like. I wonder why Mama can't be pretty like Madeline but suddenly I feel so guilty for thinking such rude thoughts I quickly pray to God for forgiveness.

"How do you know her?" Mother demands.

"She works at the library." I lie smoothly not meeting her eyes.

"Tramp." Mother mutters under her breath looking in her direction. I act like I don't hear anything because I know that Mother wouldn't want me to hear her talk like that.

Mother grabs my hand and rushes me away out of there. Protective, as always.

F

F is for flashback. Flashbacks are supposed to remind you of how things were in past. Unfortunately, sometimes they remind of us just how much the past resembles the present.

FLASHBACK

Past

"I don't wanna go! I'm scared! Daddy put me down!" I am hollering at the top of my six year old lungs. My arms are flailing and I am hanging in mid-air in daddys hands as he walks deeper and deeper into the sea.

"Daddy don't let me go!" I cry, begging almost.

I feel a shift as he loosens his grip and ignoring my desperate pleas shouts happily "swim on!" and throws me into the deep water.

Shrieking and arms flailing I feel my body plunge ~d into the oceans deep blue waters and my eyes ~orror. I feel as if I am watching from above; ~ody of a child hit the water slowly bottom of the ocean floor. Arms ~o shaken up to have a true ~ sky in need of a savior ~ddenly a wave of ~t the waters movement ~lling me up ~nd filling my ~avily my shaky on my own tears was holding me so ~s just a second ago.

"Jonathan what the hell is the matter with you!?"
I faintly hear a voice yelling at Daddy; it sounds like
Mothers voice but I had never heard her swear before
and was momentarily incapable of deciphering so
much as my own heartbeat. And within seconds I fade
back into a deep blackness.

FLASHBACK

Past

"I don't wanna go! I'm scared! Daddy put me down!" I am hollering at the top of my six year old lungs. My arms are flailing and I am hanging in mid-air in daddys hands as he walks deeper and deeper into the sea.

"Daddy don't let me go!" I cry, begging almost.

I feel a shift as he loosens his grip and ignoring my desperate pleas shouts happily "swim on!" and throws me into the deep water.

Shrieking and arms flailing I feel my body plunge toward into the oceans deep blue waters and my eyes widen in horror. I feel as if I am watching from above; watching the body of a child hit the water slowly slowly falling to the bottom of the ocean floor. Arms attempting to paddle but too shaken up to have a true direction, eyes peering up at the sky in need of a savior I struggle to stay somewhat afloat. Suddenly a wave of darkness hits and just as I am about to let the waters engulf my lungs and steal my breath I feel a movement in the water; arms grasping my legs and pulling me up up higher; breaking through the waters and filling my lungs with fresh oceanic air. Sobbing heavily my shaky arms cling onto his neck as I choke on my own tears in utter disbelief that the man who was holding me so close now had fed me to the sharks just a second ago.

"Jonathan what the hell is the matter with you!?" I faintly hear a voice yelling at Daddy; it sounds like Mothers voice but I had never heard her swear before and was momentarily incapable of deciphering so much as my own heartbeat. And within seconds I fade back into a deep blackness.

T

T is best expressed through timeliness and thoughts; the finite amount of time that we as humans are relevant on this Earth and what we choose to spend that time thinking about.

TIMELINESS

Past

Averting my eyes I scamper quickly into my haven, shutting the door softly behind. Knowing the terminable safety of my thoughts I furiously scribble them down on a page of crisp white paper ripped from a tattered notebook for only when they are translated into tangible lacings of contemplations chained with silent tears they are no longer inside of me; suffocating me; instilling dangerously radical ideas into my senses. The thoughts were safe inside my coven of secrets because He would never dare step into it; for if He did, He would see the perishable gasp within me and be overwhelmed by the realization that I was no longer an outlet; an image; an abstraction. He would comprehend that I existed outside the realm of his injustice; something his father had never realized in him. I stabbed away at the paper with the linking of my nouns and verbs; losing myself in a trance. I embraced the feeling of being nowhere, not being present on this earth, not thinking; because not thinking meant not feeling and not feeling meant achieving the esctasy of nothingness. Even if the nothingness was a deceptive lie, dressed up in elegant clothing; it was the same nothingness to me. To speak of the unspoken was unheard of to him, but not because he hadn't heard it before. I long to one day open my mouth and have the suppressed sorrows escape me and flow freely from my tongue. I will no longer be a song bird trapped inside a lion's cage; my voice will be free to ring from the depths of the oceans and the peaks of my mountains.

THOUGHTS

Judy Ryans sat at her desk with her spectacles hovering on her nose deep in thought about the piece that lie in front of her. She knew it wouldn't be long before someone as clever as Eva would figure out there was no need to be physically present at her weekly therapy sessions if the meeting normally ended in a mere exchange of papers and the occasional praise. The latest piece, just as all of them do originally, sent shivers down Mrs. Ryans back.

"Thoughts" the title glared back at her on the piece of crisp white paper.

Filling up my brain
Leaking out my ears

Following me all day
Innocently crawling into my dreams
After the sun signals for dark to come

I think thoughts all day and night
I think thoughts that take me places
I think thoughts that win me races
I think of colors and butterflies
Rocket ships and starry skies

Thoughts that take me places
Far away
And near the bay

I think up mazes and tunnels
And highways and funnels
Skywalks
And bridges
Road blocks and ridges

Thoughts that leak into my ears
Refilling up my brain

"Leave it up to the schitzo to have thoughts leaking out her ears" Judy muttered to herself as she rubbed her temple and folded the sheet of paper back in its envelope and into her bin.

S

S is for something that has alluded most of us to such a heartbreaking end that we've decided to fabricate it ourselves; significance.

SIGNIFICANCE

Humanity has known from the beginning of time that we are irreversibly doomed so we feel the need to make our significance tangible in a countless number of forms even if that means manufacturing our own significance and ultimately poisoning our existence.

As cameras flash at the creations in front of them the photographers are not actually enjoying the image; they are frantically attempting to capture it on their photo taking device. They are so lost behind their lens that they scramble to capture the essence of a series of moments for safekeeping for *later* because to them the only function of the present is to preserve everything for the future.

When one gets lost in the moment of attempting to savor something for the *future*, they forget about appreciating it in the *present*.

Instead of simply living *through* every moment be *alive* for it and *embrace* it instead.

N

N is for never.

NEVER FIND IT

The very reason we desire and fantasize about perfection is because we admire its brief and flinging touch-the way it eludes us, taunts us, and just barely escapes out from under our slippery grasp. And yet it was Oscar Wilde that once said "nowadays people know the worth of everything and the value of nothing" because they deceive themselves into thinking not only do they want to find the unknown but that they want to *unravel* it too. They convince themselves that they even want to label it with a price tag and sell it for a convenient low price at the supermarket nearest you.

Yet when soon he finds the object of his desire its innocence will be tarnished forever and as its path from extraordinary to ordinary begins it will cease to resemble his purest form of perfection.

There is only one route man could take to avoid this destruction; never find it.

C

C is for two things; one is an evil and one is a gift. What we often struggle with however is figuring which one is which?

CHANGE

People enjoy museums for reasons that are neither artistic nor intellectual. People enjoy museums not because of their supposed fascination with the history that is *preserved* so delicately but rather because of the very fact that it is preserved. The inherent human unwillingness to accept change brings us to admire and almost desire continuity. For it is only in continuity that we find stability and sanity.

To preserve something in its purest form is to ensure that it will never be altered. Even if that something can be rearranged or recreated into something better than the original that is a risk more dangerous than most of us are willing to take.

We need certainty, we need reassurance that everything will stay constant-unchanging.

CONFORMITY

We all want different ends

Never stopping to make amends

Our deepest desires

Fuel our neighbors' fastest fires

We wallow in our fears

As we swallow our own tears

But they will never know

Because we never bother to stop and show

Hiding behind our vanity

We unclothe our deepest insanity

We loathe he who breaks free

Because of our fear that he will no

longer agree

Or conform to society's trap

That sucks us in and shuts with a snap

Engulfing humanity

It slowly begins to breed our insanity

CONFUSION

As I came face to face with the beast I stared at the pale coldness within his eyes and at that moment I couldn't bring myself to feel anything. So burdened by the unbearable suffering inside of me I couldn't help but feeling remorseful, but not for myself. The beasts' eyes were intent and so focused onto my pain as if my suffering was its only happiness, its only gain, its only reason to live. But I had reached that level of nothingness; of complete and utter numbness and I wanted nothing from the world; I was finished, I was through. The only thing I yearned for was to wither slowly in front my audience and inculcate the same fear in them as they had instilled into me.

CONTUSION

As I sat in her small office overlooking the buildings of lower Manhattan I waited impatiently for the mystery woman to walk in.

"Hello Ms. Fields" a voice suddenly boomed as a beautiful young woman walked in from the back and shook my hand coolly as she sat down at her desk.

"Hello" I whispered as I crossed my legs slowly.

"Well the book is remarkable! Eva is quite a character. The way this youngin views a cruel world so full of violence so sure she will never be capable of divorcing herself away from her horrible reality—it really is quite beautiful . . . but are you sure you want to publish this?" she asked.

"Why would I not?" I ask perplexed that she would even ask such a thing.

"Because you reveal Evas deepest insecurities, her fears, and her confusion in her most vulnerable times!"

I laughed a deep laugh and grin at her, "Ma'am I think you're overreacting Eva is just a character! A figment of my imagination!"

"Oh Beatrice you're so deep in your own imagination you've failed to recognize the startling truth that's spelled out so clearly in front of you!"

"And what that might be" I swallow the rising lump in my throat not ready to have my darkest fear in the world be confirmed.

"Miss," she paused dramatically and scrunched up her eyebrows so that she is looking straight into my eyes. In that second I could feel her breath and I could see the words tumbling towards me like a runaway train derailing off its tracks everything happening at once I braced myself for the fall.

Mrs. Ryans opened her mouth to speak "you are Eva."

ABOUT THE AUTHOR

When Ella is not people watching and secretly entering her own dialogue into their conversations or lying under the sun and pondering about everything under the stars she is furiously typing away on her 1920s Underwood typewriter (which recently underwent some successful repairs thanks to Mr. Robert Wood). Ella has been writing since kindergarten—a time when she would receive a stick of red licorice and a paper crown from her principal, Mr. McKamey for every story that she wrote. What makes Ellas writing so unique is her remarkable ability to objectively illustrate every perspective within a situation—breaking the traditional mold of the good guy/bad guy dilemma so that every character is given an element of humanness—so that the words in front of her readers are not undecipherable calligraphy but rather situations that they too can relate to. Ella finds intrigue in the most simple and yet some of the most complex things in the world so that her writing is a sincere translation of her fascination of both the physical and metaphysical world around her. Ellas stories are timeless for the underlying element of social criticism in her stories ensures that for as long as society will continue manufacturing significance her words will stay relevant.